Dear Parents:

Congratulations! Your child is taking the first steps on an exciting journey. The destination? Independent reading!

STEP INTO READING® will help your child get there. The program offers five steps to reading success. Each step includes fun stories and colorful art or photographs. In addition to original fiction and books with favorite characters, there are Step into Reading Non-Fiction Readers, Phonics Readers and Boxed Sets, Sticker Readers, and Comic Readers—a complete literacy program with something to interest every child.

Learning to Read, Step by Step!

Ready to Read   **Preschool–Kindergarten**
• big type and easy words • rhyme and rhythm • picture clues
For children who know the alphabet and are eager to begin reading.

Reading with Help   **Preschool–Grade 1**
• basic vocabulary • short sentences • simple stories
For children who recognize familiar words and sound out new words with help.

Reading on Your Own   **Grades 1–3**
• engaging characters • easy-to-follow plots • popular topics
For children who are ready to read on their own.

Reading Paragraphs   **Grades 2–3**
• challenging vocabulary • short paragraphs • exciting stories
For newly independent readers who read simple sentences with confidence.

Ready for Chapters   **Grades 2–4**
• chapters • longer paragraphs • full-color art
For children who want to take the plunge into chapter books but still like colorful pictures.

STEP INTO READING® is designed to give every child a successful reading experience. The grade levels are only guides; children will progress through the steps at their own speed, developing confidence in their reading.

Remember, a lifetime love of reading starts with a single step!

Step into Reading, Random House, and the Random House colophon are registered trademarks of Penguin Random House LLC.

Visit us on the Web!
StepIntoReading.com
randomhousekids.com

Educators and librarians, for a variety of teaching tools, visit us at RHTeachersLibrarians.com

ISBN 978-1-101-93887-4 (trade) — ISBN 978-1-101-93888-1 (lib. bdg.)

Printed in the United States of America
10 9 8 7 6 5 4 3 2 1

nickelodeon

BIG TRUCK SHOW!

BUBBLE GUPPIES

by Mary Tillworth

based on the teleplay "Humunga-Truck!"
by Rodney Stringfellow

based on the TV series *Bubble Guppies,*
created by Robert Scull and Jonny Belt

cover illustrated by Steve Talkowski

interior illustrated by MJ Illustrations

Random House 🏠 New York

Honk, honk!

Beep, beep!

Here come

the trucks!

A fire truck is red.

It has a ladder.

The lights flash.

The siren is loud!

A dump truck
is full of sand.
The back goes up.
The sand slides out!

A garbage truck
takes trash away.
Pee-yew!

Gil and Molly
hold their noses!

A mail truck brings mail.

Goby gets
a letter!

It is time

for the big truck show!

The crowd
claps and cheers.

There are big trucks.
There are little trucks.

They are very
helpful trucks!

Uh-oh!
Humunga-Truck
gets stuck
in the mud!

Zoom, zoom!
Here comes
the tow truck!

The tow truck
hooks the big truck.

It pulls the big truck
out of the mud!

Hooray for trucks!

Hooray for

Humunga-Truck!